THE ADVENTURES OF
BOBBY
THE BIG RED BUS
THE JOURNEY BEGINS

BY STEVEN DONALDSON
ILLUSTRATIONS BY LISA BLARY

BIG RED BUS FACTORY

In London, England, there is a factory that makes **bright red** Double Decker buses.

Let us go inside
the factory.

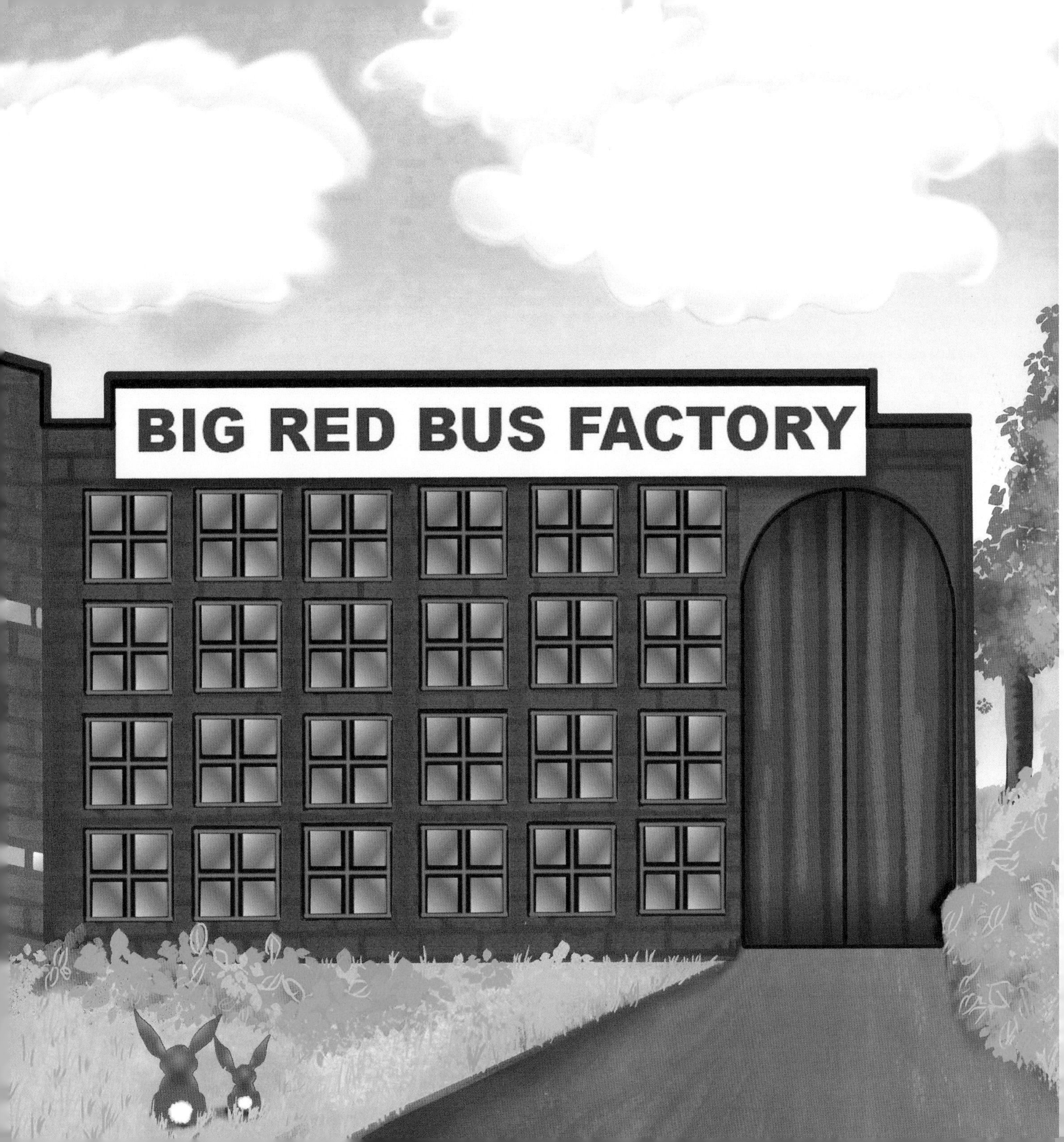
BIG RED BUS FACTORY

A double decker is a special bus. It has two floors instead of one and can carry twice as many passengers as a regular bus.

A double decker even has a staircase inside for the passengers to climb to the next level.

One fine morning, Mr Barton, the factory manager, walks up to talk to Bobby on the production line. "Good morning Bobby, glad to see things are moving along."

"Yes, I have new bright red paint and today will be getting new windows for the passengers to see through."

Mr Barton smiles and says, "Soon you will be ready to go out onto the streets of London and carry passengers all over the city."

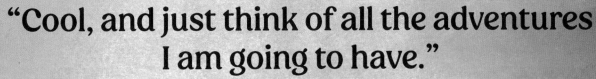

"Cool, and just think of all the adventures
I am going to have."

"Looking good, Bobby,"
says Bill the mechanic.

"Thanks, Bill, I cannot wait to see
my new windows."

"Nice windows, Bobby. You look very handsome and tomorrow you are getting your new red seats."

"Goody, new seats for the passengers."

Bobby is being fitted
with bright red seats.

"Looking good," shouts Bobby to the
workers installing his new seats.

"Bobby, here are your own licence plates. There is only one bus in the entire country with Bobby123 and that is you," says Bill.

BOBBY 123

"I love my new licence plates."

"Good morning, Beverly,
you look really great with your new shiny
windows and licence plates."

"Thanks, Bobby.
I am so excited about the graduation party!"

"Me too," says Bobby.

George the chief mechanic and his friends are having a nice cup of tea discussing tomorrow's big graduation day.

"It is going to be the best Double Decker bus graduation day ever," says George.

Bobby, Beverly and all the bright red double decker buses are graduating today.

There are banners and balloons and cake for everyone.

Mr. Barton begins his speech.

"Today I am proud to announce that you, the latest graduates, are ready to go out onto the streets of London as official London Double Decker buses.

You have passed your tests and are ready to follow in the tire tracks of all the great London Double Decker buses who have gone before you.

I will be very sad to see you go, but I know you are all excited and cannot wait to go out onto the streets of London and enjoy the many adventures that await you. I salute you."

All the workers cheer with joy.

"Hip hip hooray, hip hip hooray, hip hip hooray."

Bobby comes out of the factory gate for the first time and all the workers come to say goodbye.

"What a beautiful world out here," says Bobby.

Mr. Barton introduces Bobby
to his new conductor, Andy.

" Nice to meet you," says Andy.

"It is my pleasure," says Bobby.

Bobby picks up his first passengers.
"Hello, everybody, plenty of room upstairs."

"Bobby you did very well today and the passengers were very happy and they all said you did a great job on your first day."

"Yes, it was a lovely day and great to see the happy faces of the children when they ride in a bright red Double Decker bus," says Bobby.

"Well, time to go to sleep. Even Double Decker buses have to go to bed," says Frank.

A large blanket comes down from the ceiling covering Bobby, as he falls fast asleep. Bobby is dreaming of his next adventure.

The End

About the Author

STEVEN DONALDSON

Steven is a writer and owner of THE BIG RED BUS COMPANY in Hollywood, CA. Steven has experienced first hand the positive and genuine love for these Iconic red London Double Decker buses. Steven decided, based on his years of experience, to create a character that children worldwide could love and enjoy. And so he wrote a bedtime story. Here it is "THE ADVENTURES OF BOBBY THE BIG RED BUS."

About the Illustrator

LISA BLARY

Lisa is a French actress and artist living in Los Angeles, Lisa dedicates this, her first illustrated children's book, to her daughter Sarah, who loves bedtime stories.

ISBN: 978-1-7379747-0-3 First Printing, 2021

Printed in Great Britain
by Amazon

79379496R00020